Cassie Pup Takes the Cake??

Library of Congress Control Number: 2017912161

Publisher's Cataloging-in-Publication Data
(Provided by Cipblock.com)

Poe-Pape, Sheri
Cassie Pup Takes the Cake?? / by Sheri Poe-Pape;
illustrated by Dasguptarts

SUMMARY: In the sequel to "Cassie's Marvelous Music Lessons,"

Cassie is adopted by a new owner, a baker, who involves the playful pup in a cupcake bake off with a mischievous champion cat baker.

Audience: Ages 3-8

ISBN-13: 978-1974028153

ISBN-10: 1974028151

1. Dogs-Juvenile fiction. 2. Contests-Juvenile fiction. 3. Cupcakes-Juvenile fiction. 4. Friendship-Juvenile fiction. 5. Pet adoption-Juvenile fiction. 6. Baking-Juvenile fiction.}

P27.P75155Ca 2017   {E}
                        Dc23

Book Information: www.sheripoe-pape.com

Sheri Poe-Pape has written many internet and newspaper articles about people in the arts and history and has been the Director/Educator of the Pape Conservatory of Music for the past thirty-eight years. She is the author of two childrens' picture books, the Award-winning Cassie's Marvelous Music Lessons and Cassie Pup takes the Cake?? Each day, she warms up on the piano, and for fifteen of those years, a small dog has been her constant companion.

In recent years, little Cassie has stood on the right side of the keyboard and brushed the author's hands off the keys—a habit that inspired the first book! Cassie's love of helping Sheri bake inspired her second book Cassie Pup takes the Cake?? The author is a graduate of Northern Illinois University where she studied Music, English, and Creative Writing. She lives with her family in northern Illinois, where she continues to write and to teach music—alongside Cassie.

The illustrator, Sudipta Dasgupta, is an experienced commercial artist. He has been in this profession for the past seven years after graduating from Gov't College of Art and Craft, Kolkata, India with 1st Class marks, and is comfortable with any style and medium. He is the owner of Dasguptarts, and has extensive experience creating artwork in a variety of styles and mediums for over one hundred and twenty companies and individuals world-wide. He does drawing and painting in all mediums, digital and traditional. His artworks have been created for storybooks and other books, book covers, cartoons, caricatures, image editing, comic strips, advertising elements, storyboard, poster, web pages, dangler, POS design, magazine ads, press ads, show cards, greeting cards, games, mobile apps, calendars, logo design, pavilion design, etc. The variety and quality of his artwork can be seen at http://www.dasguptarts.com and he can be reached at the same web address.

To the golden-haired boy of my youth

Cassie Pup Takes the Cake??

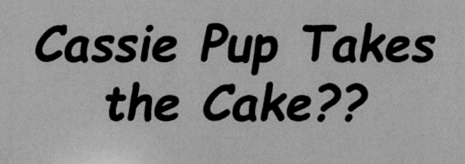

Sheri Poe-Pape

Illustrated by Dasguptarts

Printed by Create Space

Chapter 1

Cassie Pup is being adopted into her new home today! The bakery shop glistens like whipped topping. The revolving door smells like cotton candy.

"Welcome Cassie!" cheers Baker Bindi.

Baker Bindi's hat is shaped like a puffy biscuit on top. Her hair is reddish brown. Her smile is the widest Cassie has ever seen. Good afternoon, Baker Bindi, Cassie is thinking as she enters the shop. She continues to softly bark to Baker Bindi as she thinks ... *I am chosen as your new doggie baking helper. I am known as the 'Best Barking Baker.' I am also known to make the yummiest 'Secret Recipe Fizzy Melt-in-your-Mouth Gumdrop Cupcakes.' Kindly show me to your kitchen!!*

"Right this way," says Baker Bindi.

"Right-o," Cassie woofs.

Baker Bindi leads Cassie through the door - *swoosh* - to her cupcake kitchen. The oven is hot. The chocolate/cherry batters flow from a little revolving fountain. Nearby are many colorful frostings of peach, purple plus yellow. They are already sparkling like little fireworks!

Cassie is bouncing on all fours, slap-slap-slap! Her stubby tail is wagging. Her milk-chocolate eyes are twinkling. She is sure her new owner will understand why she is happy. She is going to be baking!

With my new super-duper haircut, perky ears with blueberry bow, I am sure to be a lean, queen bakery machine, oh yeah! she giggles to herself.

"This is for you, Cassie," announces Baker Bindi.
"It is your own baker's hat with apron!"

Cassie excitedly puts them on. They
are green with little cherry muffins
stitched on them. *I am proud of
these*, glows Cassie. She does a
diggity-dog dance while barking
"doo-doo-a-doodley-doo-awoooooo!"

Chapter 2

"Here we have Cordelia Cat," says Baker Bindi. "She is known for her 'World's Best Upside-Down Right-Side-Up Cupcakes.' One must lap up the middle frosting of her cupcakes quickly with a straw before they explode like fiery wildflowers," she adds.

"Greetings Baker Bindi, greetings Cassie," meows Cordelia. She is also sure Baker Bindi along with Cassie will understand she is a happy baker too! *I would never have a "hisssssy" fit about baking with anyone,* she playfully thinks.

Cordelia Cat resembles any other cat, except her stripes are brightly orange. Her red licorice smile highlights her small marshmallow-shaped teeth. She also wears a brown baker's hat with apron. The apron is weaved with rainbow-dyed swirls of yarn.

Cordelia Cat is not any ordinary cupcake kitty. She is known by *Meow News* and the world as the "Cat's Meow." You see, she never loses a baking contest!

"What a howl to meet you, Cordelia," softly squeals Cassie.

"It would have been a cat-astrophe not to bake together," Cordelia purrs slyly.

"Ready to start, Cordelia?" barks Cassie.

"You may cat-apult me to the cupcake batter," playfully hisses Cordelia.

Cassie feels ready. *I always win these baking contests. This will be a cinch to win*, she daydreams too proudly.

Cassie's cupcakes are especially tasty. They have one simple problem though. One must take the first bite carefully to keep the *fizz* from getting out of hand.

An audience of bakery customers gather around the pair.
There is excitement in the air. Baker Bindi times her music box watch
chim-chime. "Are we ready to bake?" she shouts. "Steady ready,"
echoes Cassie, holding her willow spoon dipped in her cherry-battered bowl
"Purr-fect to go," sighs Cordelia. "Okay, countdown - 5...4...3...2...1...
let the baking begin!" shouts Baker Bindi.

Chapter 3

They're off!! Both peppermint-scented cake mixers are spinning side by side. The contestants never take their eyes off one another.

"I can bake plus frost my fizzy cupcakes faster than you can," boasts Cassie.

"I'm sure I have no time for talking or a *Pat-a-Cake, Pat-a-Cake, Baker's Man* with you," brags Cordelia. "You can bet I will leave you in a fog with my explosive cake and frosting."

"Hmmm, we shall see," Cassie howls. "Or, should I say, we shall *taste?*"

The contestants speed up their cupcake beating, with each struggling to hold on to their bowls.

"Keep your stirring on your side of the oven!" screeches Cassie.

"You are the one on my side of the true cupcake counter!" screams Cordelia.

Without warning, both the peppermint-scented cake mixers spin totally out of control, making the bowls clank together!

"Holy spumoni! If they come loose we will be covered as one big cupcake!" hollers Baker Bindi.

Both bowls of batter zig-zag around each other. In a split second, they collide like a Fourth of July explosion! The batter not only splashes the ceiling, it is all over the three unhappy bakers plus the audience!

"It is all your fault! You interfered with my baking!" shrieks Cordelia.

"Aaaaah! I guess some invisible man wrecked *my* bowl of batter, huh?" yells Cassie.

"Honestly, *both* of your crazy stirrings created this messy disaster," declares Baker Bindi. "Unfortunately, this behavior means neither of you will win the baking contest."

"Whaaaat?" shout Cassie along with Cordelia, staring at each other in horror.

"If you both had not been greedy trying to win a contest, this would have turned out okay," says Baker Bindi.

I only wanted to prove that I am still the 'Best Barking Baker.' What a disaster! Cassie thinks to herself.

Cordelia Cat is thinking harshly to herself too. *There goes my title of the 'Cat's Meow'! What will Meow News and the world think of me?*

"If only we had not stirred like crazy," Cassie moans sadly. "Our Upside-Down Right-Side-Up Melt-in-your-Mouth Gumdrop Cupcake mixture would not have become an accident."

"I have learned that I cannot always win each contest," growls Cassie.
"Yes," softly whispers Cordelia. "This is a hard lesson about losing, about being a good loser. Most important is we learned to forgive, to show peace between each other."

"I agree. Say, how about a future adventure together?" howls Cassie.
"Will it be in baking?" meows Cordelia.
"We will have to see, my friend," Cassie yelps as she winks a big wink.
"We will have to wait to see."

 Watch for more Cassie books. Be sure to also get "Cassie's Marvelous Music Lessons," winner of a 2013 Midwest Publishing Awards Show Award and a 2017 Hungry Monster Silver Literary award.
Available through Amazon and Barnes and Noble.

"Cassie Pup Takes the Cake?" available through Amazon, Barnes and Noble and Books a Million.

D. Donovan, Senior Editor- Midwest Book Review -
"Young readers with good reading skills or adults looking for an especially lively read-aloud will find Cassie Pup Takes the Cake?? an inviting, fun story of responsibility, competition, and friendship in a new Cassie Pup adventure highly recommended for adults who look for leisure stories about animal friends and lessons about how friendships are built."

46340781R00020

Made in the USA
Middletown, DE
27 May 2019